W   tty?

This is my first Dotty book and I hope to
write many more about the adventures we
have together. I want to thank my family and
friends who have encouraged me
with this endeavor.

Photography and words:
Peggy Powell

Dotty Illustrations:
Denis Sazhin, US
from the Noun Project

Design by Matt Strelecki

Peggy Powell

Dotty

♡ Thanks to Elizabeth Byrd
(Betty) Hazen for helping get
Dotty's first book published.

Aunt Betty is one of
Dotty's biggest fans.

Red and yellow
flowers are growing
in the pot.

Is Dotty in the pot
as well?
No, she is not.

Leaves have fallen
all over the town.

Both Dotty and foliage
are yellow and brown.

Moose the yellow lab is
peeking through the glass.

Look again! There's Dotty, a
tiny little lass.

In the toy box there is a
llama, monkey, snake...

You can see Dotty in
the center if you do a
double take.

Snow has drifted all around,
so beautiful
and white.

Dotty hurries to her home,
she does not like frostbite.

Doggy toys and
treats abound.

Can you find the
spotted hound?

A blanket with a dog
pattern looks so very soft.

One of the dogs is Dotty,
her nose and head aloft.

Beautiful trees and nature
surrounding a small lake,

Walking along rocks is
Dotty- or is that a spotted
snake?!

Laundry basket
spilling, with clothes no
longer clean

Shirts and socks
and towels, with Dotty
in between.

A little silver car, but
no one is inside,

Oh wait, now I see Dotty!
She's ready for a ride.

Is that Dotty in a movie on
the television screen?

No, but she is watching from
the chair, quiet
and serene.

Ringo wears a blue collar,
he's laying on his head.

Do you see where he lays,
Dotty is his bed!

Brown and yellow leaves,
swirling in the air,

In the shadow of
the tree, it's Dotty standing
there.

Five pillows white
and colored, all sitting
on a bed.

If you look a little
closer, you will see
Dotty's head.

In a lovely garden,
the vegetable plants
are green.

Is it even possible for Dotty
to be seen?

Campfire flames are
flickering with orangish-red
and yellow.

Do you see where
Dotty is? She's toasting
a marshmallow.

Under the blanket
fringe, I see a spotted little
snoot.

It looks like our friend
Dotty is wearing a
ghillie suit!

There is an old, covered
bridge of burgundy
and white.

If you look a little closer,
Dotty is in sight.

A cozy little house, inside
the lights aglow,

Is Dotty in or out?
It's difficult to know.

Gladiolas growing—
colorful, bright
and tall,

Dotty stands amongst them,
the flowers
make her small.

Going for a bike ride
on a sunny summer day,

Dotty's nowhere to be
found, but her shadow's
on display.

Do you see Dotty swimming
in the Gulf of Mexico?

No, you can't see her
swimming, but you can
probably see a toe!

Lying on the green grass,
Dotty you can find.

But did you see the
dragonfly, sitting on
her behind?

About the author:
Peggy Powell is a retired school
counselor and teacher.

In addition to Dotty, Peggy is the mom of twin sons,
Levi and Josh, both engineers living in Durham, North
Carolina. She is also mom to her daughter, Molly, a
second-grade teacher
in Eddyville, Iowa.

Peggy and Dotty live in Johnston, Iowa with Dotty's
dad, Bill. The three of them love to ride bikes, kayak,
travel and garden together.

Made in the USA
Middletown, DE
31 March 2021